The Cold Heart of Summer

by

Alan Gibbons

First published 2002 in Great Britain by Barrington Stoke Ltd
10 Belford Terrace, Edinburgh EH4 3DQ
Copyright © 2002 Alan Gibbons

The moral right of the author has been asserted in
accordance with the Copyright, Designs and
Patents Act 1988

ISBN 1-84299-080-2

Printed by Polestar AUP Aberdeen Ltd

A Note from the Author

We are all haunted, by our memories, by our dreams, by our nightmares. I grew up in the Cheshire countryside around a village called Whitegate. There I saw ghosts between the trees and in the mist on the water at New Pool and Petty Pool where I played. It doesn't really matter whether they were there or not. I wanted them to be there.

When I was very young my father had a terrible accident and was unable to carry on working as a farm labourer. We had to move from the country to a nearby town. Suddenly I was haunted, not by my imaginary ghosts, but by a sense of loss. Instead of the lush countryside, I had to play in the backstreets of Crewe. I took refuge in stories – in books from the library and the black-and-white movies on TV. One movie, *Dead of Night*, featured a haunted mirror. That was the seed that later grew into *The Cold Heart of Summer*.

To all at Prescot County Primary
and Simonswood

Contents

Chapter 1
Born Evil

Nobody is born evil, that's what people say.

"But what about houses?" Debbie spoke the thought aloud.

"Did you say something?" asked Dad.

"No," said Debbie.

But I should say something, she thought. *I should say something now, before he takes this job doing up the house. Go on, say it loud and clear. Leave this place and don't ever come back. The only thing that was ever at home here is terror.*

But she didn't say anything. She just stood there beside her dad and looked up at the windows of the house. There were eyes looking down at her. But who did they belong to?

"Are you OK, Debbie?" Dad said.

"Yes. Why do you ask?"

"I don't know. You seem so jumpy. Is it your exams?"

"Could be," she said.

You can think what you like, Dad, she thought to herself. *I am worried about the results of my exams. I've got boyfriend trouble. Take your pick. There's no way I can tell you what I'm really feeling.*

"It'll need a lot of work done on it," said Dad.

Debbie nodded.

"The house is little more than a shell," he went on.

Yes, but just think what can live in a shell.

"What's it going to be used for, offices or something?" Debbie asked.

"No – it's going to be somebody's home. The woman who's bought it comes from London. She must have money to burn, that's all I can say. Fancy doing up a shell like this."

Someone from London. It makes sense, thought Debbie. *Nobody from round these parts would think of moving in here.*

"You're spooked, aren't you?" said Dad. "You believe all the evil stories about the place."

Debbie looked up at the Grange.
She believed it was evil all right, but not
because of the stories. It was because of
what she was feeling now this moment.
There was a blade of ice right there in her
heart. She knew why too. It was because the
house was looking down at her, sizing her up,
deciding what to do with her.

"Let's have a look inside," said Dad.

"A house that was born evil," she said,
when Dad was far enough away.

Born evil.

Chapter 2
The Cold

Once they were inside the house, Debbie started to feel even worse. It was a hot August day but she felt cold, so cold. It was as if it was August for everyone else, but not for her.

For Debbie it was deepest winter. "Are you cold, too?" she asked.

"Cold? Are you kidding?" Dad replied. "It's the hottest summer in years, a real scorcher. You must be coming down with flu or something."

There he goes again, Debbie thought, *coming up with an easy answer. Why can't he see the real reason? I'm cold because the house is cold, cold deep down inside.*

"This job is really too much for Billy and me," said Dad. "I could do with more help. But we'll just have to manage. I can't afford to pay anyone else."

Billy was Dad's mate. They had worked together for years.

Suddenly Debbie felt lost. She wanted to scream and shout, to tell Dad not to take this job. But how could she? They needed the money badly. Dad's business was heading for the rocks, and fast.

It had all started when Mum died. He just couldn't cope any more. For months he hardly worked at all. By the time he got started again, nobody wanted to take him on any more. They couldn't trust him.

"You need this job, don't you, Dad?"

"You bet I do. Without it, we're in deep trouble. They could even take our house away to pay the debts off."

Then Debbie got that feeling again, the feeling of being helpless and alone. How could she tell Dad to walk away from this job? What reason could she give? Because she was feeling cold? That was just so stupid.

"Could we really lose our house?" she asked.

Dad nodded.

"You should see how much money I owe. It's scary."

It wasn't nearly as scary as the Grange. Nothing was that scary.

A car's horn blared outside.

"That'll be Billy," said Dad. "You have a look round. I'll be back in a moment."

She watched him bounding downstairs. She wanted to run after him, but it would look silly. She was 16, after all, old enough to go out to work.

But she was still young enough to be scared out of her skin by something she couldn't see, by the cold in the marrow of her bones. *No, I'll be brave*, thought Debbie.

Turning left along the landing, she saw a door standing partly open. Inside, something caught her eye. It was a flash of light, then a movement.

She took a step towards the room. Then she stopped. "What am I doing?" she said, her voice echoing across the landing.

Had she seen too many scary films? 'Don't', she always used to tell the girl in the film, 'Don't go through that door'. So right now Debbie didn't go into the room.

Taking care to keep her face turned away so she wouldn't see anything bad, she stepped forward and slowly closed the door.

Chapter 3

Sexton

Dad didn't come back for ages. In the end Debbie went to find him. He was outside, at the front of the house.

"Hi there, Debbie," said Billy, Dad's mate. "Taking a good look round?"

Debbie gave a thin smile. "Something like that," she said.

"I'll go and pick up this lot then," said Billy. "I'll call in at the builder's yard on the way home."

He put the list of building materials in his pocket and drove off in his battered flatbed truck.

"Don't the stories people tell about the house bother you at all?" Debbie said to her dad.

"What, the ones about old man Sexton?" he asked.

Debbie nodded. "After all, he's the most famous murderer for miles around."

"Sexton doesn't worry me," said Dad. "He's been dead for seventy years."

"Yes, I know he's dead," said Debbie. "But he won't lie down. The Grange has been standing empty most of that time. Everyone gets scared away. They never stay long."

"Just because of some crazy old man," said Dad. "Crazy, piggy-eyed Sexton."

He stood in front of the house. "Are you up there?" he shouted.

"Don't do that, Dad," said Debbie.

Dad took no notice. "Are you up there?" he called. "Hey, Mr Sexton, crazy, piggy-eyed Sexton!"

"Dad, stop it."

"He can't hear us, love," said Dad. "Or can you, you barmy old goat?"

He started to sing softly, the same silly rhyme they'd been singing around here for years, ever since they locked Sexton away.

Sexton, Sexton, tell us your secret do,
Piggy-eyed and crazy,
We all of us know it was you!

All at once the song stuck in his throat. He sprang to one side, pushing Debbie away. A whole window frame had fallen out and smashed onto the ground. Splinters of wood and slivers of broken glass flew around like darts.

It was a moment before either of them spoke.

Then Dad said, "Those frames are more rotten than I thought! I'd better rip them out."

Debbie looked up at the hole in the wall where the window had been. She counted the windows. The loose frame had come from the room where she had seen movement.

She breathed a sigh of relief that she hadn't gone in.

Chapter 4

First Blood

Debbie didn't want to go back to the house, but she'd promised Dad and Billy that she would get them some fish and chips.

She couldn't think of any excuse for not going back to the old house either. Her best friend Lisa was away on holiday with her parents. As for John, well, Debbie didn't have a boyfriend any more. He had called her father a loser and nobody got away with that.

"Dad? Billy?" she called up from outside the front door.

What Debbie really wanted was for them to come down and get their fish and chips. She didn't want to go inside. Someone or something was waiting for her in there.

"Dad?" she called out again.

The word stuck in her throat. She was already starting to panic. *It was crazy. Dad and Billy were probably on their way down the stairs that minute.*

She began to imagine that something awful might have happened. "Where are you, Dad?" she yelled again.

The front door was wide open. *Why keep it closed? After all, there was nothing to steal. Everything that had been inside the house was now piled in the skip.*

"I've got your fish and chips."

She heard knocking, even louder than the knocking of her heart. Dad and Billy were hammering away somewhere. *So the house hadn't swallowed them up.*

"Ugh," she said. "I wish I wasn't so scared."

The knocking was coming from upstairs. There was nothing for it. She would have to go in. But the moment she stepped inside, Debbie felt that terrible cold again.

She walked across the floor. Cold. Then she touched the banister. Cold. It was all so cold that it seemed to strike right into the marrow of her bones.

She started up the stairs. Already she was shivering with that awful icy chill. It was like a claw scraping away inside her skin.

"Oh – stop it, Debbie. You're the one doing this." She had said it aloud.

"Talking to yourself?" It was only Billy, but it gave her such a violent shock that she almost tripped and fell. He was standing at the top of the stairs. "Did I scare you?"

"I didn't expect to see you there, that's all."

It wasn't all, but she was happy to have found someone, happy not to be alone.

****

"Your dad's in there," said Billy, pointing.

They were standing outside the room where she'd seen movement. It was the one with the missing window.

"In there?"

"Yes. Is something wrong?" asked Billy.

"No, of course not." Debbie led the way into the room and gave a yelp. It wasn't a scream, just a scared, little yelp. She felt stupid.

"That's what I did this morning when I came in here," said Dad. "I nearly jumped out of my skin. Fancy being scared of your own reflection."

"What's a mirror doing in here?" said Debbie. "I thought all the old stuff was in the skip."

"It is," said Dad, munching a chip. "This one is fixed to the wall. I left it up in case somebody wanted it."

"Who'd want that?" Debbie asked.

"It's a perfectly good mirror," said Dad.

Not to Debbie. It was an eye, another eye that was sizing her up, deciding what to do with her. "Who were the last owners?" Debbie asked Dad. "When were they last here?"

"Twenty years ago. They were a young couple. Everyone thought they were really happy, then one day the husband just went crazy."

"How?"

"He tried to beat his wife's brains out. He would have done it but the postman walked in and stopped him."

"But that's what old Sexton did! He beat a girl's brains out."

"That's what they say he did. But the maid's body was never found. Maybe she just ran off."

Debbie shivered. "I don't know how you can work in this place," she said. "It gives me the creeps."

It was true. Just then her flesh was creeping. The tiny hairs on her neck were standing up on end. Her whole body was telling her to go, to get out.

Go! Get out, before the same thing happens to you.

Chapter 5
The Girl in the Lake

Debbie got out of the house, but she didn't go far. Dad and Billy were almost done. If she hung around for half an hour, she would be able to get a lift home.

"Debbie girl," she said to herself, "You're cracking up."

She glanced back at the Grange. Through the trees she saw the windows. Small, bright eyes were staring at her. Piggy eyes.

"Crazy old Sexton," Debbie said, "with his piggy, piggy eyes."

But she said it very softly, just in case he was listening. She carried on through the trees, keen to get out of sight of the Grange.

At last she was well away from there. She found herself walking along the banks of a lake.

So this is Grange Mere. What a beautiful lake. Why haven't I been here before?

Debbie wondered for a moment why nobody seemed to know about it. Then she understood. The motorway was on one side and the ring road on the other. The only way down to the lake was through the grounds of the Grange.

For the first time that day there was a breath of wind. It blew against her face and her T-shirt. She shut her eyes.

Then something hit her face. Icy needles pricked her skin. It was there again, that cold feeling. It bit into her and penetrated her bones.

"No!" Debbie shouted, though there was no-one there.

It wasn't easy but she forced her eyes open. Everything was as it should be. Flies buzzed over the water. Bees hummed in the bushes. It was summer. But for a moment, while her eyes had been closed, it had been winter.

I think I'm going crazy.

A moment later, she knew she was. A few metres out from a crumbling, old landing-stage pier, she had a brief glimpse of her reflection in the water. It was her, but she was different. Her hair was scraped back under a white cap and she was wearing a black dress and white apron.

Debbie scooped up a handful of dirt and gravel and threw it at the reflection in the water. When the ripples faded, she saw herself once more, this time in her blue T-shirt and jeans again.

"Weird."

Chapter 6
The Fall

Debbie glanced at her watch. It was almost time to go back. Time to get back to the Grange and get that lift. She hurried through the woods, glad to leave the lake behind.

As she drew closer to the Grange, she started walking more slowly. *Why am I in such a hurry?* she thought.

Why indeed? The Grange had come into view. The Grange with its hateful, empty eyes.

"I don't know what you're playing at," she said, looking up at the windows. "You and your stupid tricks at the lake. But I'm not scared. Go on, do your worst."

She wished she hadn't said that. She had a feeling the worst the Grange could do was very bad indeed.

"Hi there, Debbie."

It was Billy. He was up a ladder, his arms reaching up to take a window frame from Dad. Dad was on the windowsill, lowering the frame carefully down to Billy.

Debbie remembered what she'd just said to the house – *go on, do your worst.*

You idiot, Debbie. Quick, you've got to get him down!

"Billy!" she shouted.

"You'll have to wait a moment or two, Debbie. I'm in a bit of a difficult position."

Please. I didn't mean it. Don't hurt him. Debbie pleaded with the house.

The house didn't hear her. Or else, it didn't listen.

Somehow, Dad lost his grip on the frame. Or maybe Billy's hands slipped. Billy tumbled back off the ladder. The window frame came after him, striking the ladder on the way down.

"Billy!" yelled Debbie.

He hit the ground hard, but he wasn't badly hurt. Not right away. It was the window frame falling onto him that did the damage. A moment after he hit the ground, a long sliver of broken glass cut into his leg. Billy's scream shattered the drowsy afternoon.

****

The ambulance came in minutes.

"You'll be OK, Billy," said Dad. "I'll follow you down to the hospital in the car."

Debbie heard something in her father's voice. Was he angry?

"He'll be all right, won't he?" Dad was asking the ambulance crew.

"Let's get him to the hospital as quick as we can, sir," said the driver.

As the ambulance drove away, Dad grabbed Debbie by the arm. He pushed her roughly towards the car. "Get in."

He *was* angry.

"Dad, you're hurting me!" protested Debbie.

"Why did you have to speak to him?" her dad demanded.

"I was trying to warn him."

"Warn him!" said Dad. "About what? A teenage girl sticking her nose in where it's not wanted?"

Her eyes stung. "Dad, that's not fair."

They were following the ambulance onto the main road.

"Tell that to Billy."

"It wasn't me who made him fall," said Debbie.

"Well, you didn't help."

She looked at him. His face looked hard. His jaw was set and his eyes ... Yes, his *eyes*.

The rhyme ran though her mind again.

Sexton, Sexton, tell us your secret do,
Piggy-eyed and crazy,
We all of us know it was you!

Piggy-eyed Sexton.

Chapter 7

The Reflection

It was two days before Debbie went near the Grange again. She was going to meet Dad there at five o'clock. They were going to Gran's for tea. One thing was for certain, when she got there she wasn't going to call up at him, not after what happened to Billy.

Instead, Debbie walked through the hallway. The moment she touched the banister it happened again, that stabbing cold. She snatched her hand away. It didn't make much difference. Her breath was frosting in front of her face.

This really can't be happening, Debbie thought.

But it was. She wasn't imagining it. Just as she hadn't imagined that reflection. Just as she hadn't imagined the way the house looked at her. This winter chill in the middle of the summer was real.

Dad's voice echoed along the landing. "Is someone there?"

There was no anger in his voice. Maybe he had at last forgiven her.

"It's only me."

"In here, Debbie."

Thank goodness. He sounded almost cheerful. He was in the room with the mirror. She kept her head turned away from the reflection. Since that moment by the lake she had kept her eyes away from glass and water.

You might see something you didn't want to see.

"Hi there, love. Look, I just wanted to say sorry I was so angry. I don't know what came over me. It's like I had someone else in my head. Crazy. What happened to Billy wasn't your fault. It was an accident, that's all."

No, thought Debbie, *it wasn't an accident*.

"It's just … you know, Billy having to take time off just when I needed an extra pair of hands. He's going to be all right by the way. Nothing broken and no major nerve or muscle damage."

"I'm glad."

"Yes, me too. Now just hang on a moment while I get myself cleaned up in the bathroom."

****

Debbie knelt down and looked at the skirting boards. Dad had almost finished replacing them. She wasn't really interested. It was just a way of keeping her eyes away from the mirror and what she might see in it.

"By the way," said Dad, calling from the bathroom. "Did I tell you what I found in that cupboard?"

"No."

"Take a look."

Debbie opened the built-in cupboard and froze. Leaning in the corner was a walking stick. It was highly polished. It was also tipped with metal, silver maybe.

"Can you see it?" called out Dad.

"Yes."

"Read what it says on the handle."

Debbie twisted the stick round and read —
JAMES SEXTON

This has got to be some sort of joke,
thought Debbie.

Dad appeared at the door. He was wearing
a fresh, white T-shirt. "Why would his stick
still be here?" he said. "It does seem odd.
The house has had four owners since Old Man
Sexton lived here."

"And didn't you throw out all the stuff in
the skip?" Debbie asked.

"Yes, I cleared out this very cupboard
myself. I would have noticed it."

"You'd think so."

"Oh well," said Dad. "I'll just have a shave and then I'll be with you."

Debbie glanced round at him in his white T-shirt. Then she caught sight of a reflection in the mirror. It was just a sleeve she saw, but that was enough. It was the sleeve of a brown tweed jacket.

Chapter 8

The Face in the Mirror

Don't look, Debbie told herself, *just don't look*.

She turned her back on the mirror and listened to the sounds of Dad shaving.

Don't look, she thought to herself again.

So she didn't look. She kept her eyes fixed on the open door.

Come on, Debbie, you'll be out of here in a minute. Keep your cool.

But keeping her cool depended on things staying normal, and they didn't.

She was just listening to Dad humming as he wiped the shaving foam off his face.

Then she saw it. "Oh my God!" she gasped.

The walking stick was leaning against the wall by the door.

But it was in the cupboard, she told herself.

"Dad, did you move the walking stick?" she called.

"No, why?" he said.

"Because it's moved!"

"It can't have."

But Debbie knew it had.

She glanced round. Shock hit her like a punch in the chest.

It was her again, the girl from the lake.

In the rippling water, Debbie had thought it was her own reflection, only in different clothes.

She had been wrong. It was another girl, about her own age. She looked terrified, just like Debbie herself. "Who are you?" Debbie asked.

The girl put a finger to her lips. Then, behind her in the mirror, the door started to open. Debbie saw the tweed sleeve, then a hand closing round the handle of the walking stick. She saw the stick being raised above the girl's head. Debbie screamed.

****

Dad came running into the room. "Debbie, what's wrong?"

"The mirror, Dad. Look in the mirror."

He did. "I don't see anything," he said.

Debbie looked again. He was right. All she saw was herself and Dad. "But I saw ..."

"What?" asked Dad.

"Oh Dad, I don't know."

She looked around for the walking stick. "Now where's it gone?"

Dad walked over to the cupboard. "Looking for this?" he said.

The walking stick was propped up in the corner of the cupboard, just where it had been when she first saw it.

Chapter 9

Rage

Debbie stayed away from the Grange for as long as she could. But she couldn't stay away forever.

Four days later she forgot her house keys. She was on her way home from the new shopping centre when she discovered this.

"Oh great," she said when she found they were missing. She looked at her watch. It was two o'clock. Either she went to the Grange or she hung around outside their house for three hours, waiting for Dad to finish work.

Looks like I've got no choice, she thought.

Twenty minutes later she was walking up the drive to the Grange. The first thing she saw was Andrea's car. "It just gets worse!" she groaned.

Andrea was Dad's new squeeze. *She* called herself that! Andrea just set Debbie's teeth on edge. All that make-up. And that voice! And the way she cooed over Dad. Ugh! *How could Dad replace Mum with somebody like her?*

Debbie was so cross that she almost forgot to feel cold. She was halfway upstairs when she felt that icy bite.

40

"Dad, it's me."

"Oh hi," he shouted down to her.

He didn't sound pleased to see her. *I bet I know why*, she thought. She found him with Andrea in the attic brewing up tea.

"Hello, Debs," said Andrea.

Debs! Only her friends called her that. Andrea was no friend. Debbie grunted something back.

"We were just having a bite to eat," said Dad. "Do you want something?"

"No thanks, I ate at that new sandwich bar."

"Could you bring our salads over?"

Debbie looked at Dad and Andrea sitting there side by side. They were like two naughty school kids. *Grow up, the pair of you!*

Debbie put the plates down in front of them.

Dad went to get a couple of cans of Coke. "Do you want one, Debbie?"

Debbie never got to answer. Andrea gave a shrill cry.

"What's wrong?" asked Debbie.

"Cockroaches. Ugh, I think I'm going to be sick."

Debbie stared. Andrea was right. Her whole plate was heaving with the things.

Dad glared at her.

"You don't think I had something to do with this!" said Debbie.

Andrea ran out of the room. Debbie heard her high-heeled shoes clattering down the wooden stairs.

"Andrea, come back!" Dad shouted after her.

A moment later Andrea's car roared and she drove off.

Debbie glanced down at the salad. The cockroaches had gone.

****

Debbie watched Dad standing on the driveway staring after Andrea.

She watched him turn. When she saw his eyes she shuddered. *They weren't his eyes. They didn't belong to the father she loved. They were piggy eyes, eyes full of hate. They were eyes cold with anger. They were like the eyes of this terrible house.*

"The house has got you, hasn't it?" she said.

She heard Dad running up the stairs. She met him on the landing.

"Dad, it wasn't me."

"No," he said. "It never is, is it?"

"But it wasn't. Where would I get cockroaches from? How could I bring myself to touch them? You know how I feel about bugs."

Dad ignored her. "I know how you feel about Andrea. But putting cockroaches in her salad! I didn't think you would stoop so low." Dad glared at her.

"Dad, listen to me. I didn't do it. I wouldn't do a thing like that."

But he didn't listen. He was looking at her with those piggy eyes. "I'm going to teach you a lesson," he said.

He came closer.

"Dad, what are you doing?" said Debbie.

Was he going to hit her? Dad had never touched her …

"Something I should have done years ago," he snarled.

He came right up to her and raised his hand to hit her.

"Dad, no!" she yelled.

She flinched, throwing up an arm to defend herself. And then she saw his face change.

He stared first at her, then at his own hand. "What am I doing? Good God, what's wrong with me?"

The look in his eyes softened. He was his old self again. "Forgive me, Debbie. I don't know what came over me."

"There's nothing to forgive," she said.

You weren't the one trying to hurt me. It was someone else.

Chapter 10

The Voice in the Room

Debbie left Dad working and walked to the library. "Let's see what I can find out about you, Mr Piggy-Eyes Sexton," she said.

In the cool, quiet rooms of the library she found out a lot.

There was the story of James Sexton himself, of course. The next-door neighbours – and they were quite far away – heard loud screams coming from the house one night in 1932. It was bitterly cold that January. Grange Mere froze over. When the police arrived they found James Sexton in the grounds of the Grange. His tweed suit was covered in blood. His eyes were staring. What's more, the maid Jane Lawson was gone. Nobody ever found her.

There was a photo of the police smashing the ice to drag the Mere for the body. Their efforts did not turn anything up.

From that night on, James Sexton never spoke another word. He was locked away in a mental hospital. He died fifty years later, taking his silence to the grave.

But the stories didn't end there. One of the owners of the Grange died a violent death. Another was almost killed. They were both women. Still others moved out, afraid for their lives.

Or their sanity.

Debbie was about to go when she remembered something. Of course, the walking stick. She had seen it raised in the mirror. She didn't remember any mention of it. She re-read the articles. No, there was no mention of the walking stick.

"So, the police never found it. They never took it away."

Armed with this knowledge she walked back to the house.

****

She ran upstairs to tell Dad what she had found out. She didn't find him in the kitchen or any of the rooms. There was one room she didn't check, of course. She stood outside the room with the mirror and called in. "Dad, are you in there?"

She heard a bump. "Dad?" she shouted.

Then there was a man's voice. It was muffled. *What was he doing?*

"Come in," said the voice.

She pushed open the door and went in. "Dad, you've got to listen to th ..."

Her voice broke off. The room was empty. She turned in panic, but the door slammed behind her. She grabbed the door handle. It was so cold it burned. She pulled her hand away and looked at the red sores on her palm.

"Dad, help me!"

Then she heard the man's voice again. "There's nobody in the house. Just you and me, Jane."

Jane? thought Debbie.

"I'm not Jane," she said.

"Don't play games with me, girl. You're a lazy, good-for-nothing child. It's time I taught you some respect," said the voice.

"Where are you?"

"Wouldn't you like to know?"

Then Debbie saw herself in the mirror. She seemed to be alone in the room and she was wearing the dress, apron and bonnet she had seen reflected in the Mere.

In panic she looked round for the walking stick. It wasn't in the cupboard. It was nowhere in the room.

So where was it?

A horrible thought came into her mind. *No, this wasn't Dad.*

"Please," she begged.

"That's it," the man's voice said. "Plead. Beg. I like that."

Then suddenly the door swung open.

Chapter 11
The Silent Scream

Debbie raced along the landing. *Why has he let me go*, she wondered. She didn't really care. She just wanted to find her dad.

"Dad. DAD! Where are you?" she shouted down the landing.

There wasn't a sound in the house. There was no knocking, no hammering.

Where was he? She ran to see if his van was still outside. She was sure she had seen it on the way in. Yes, there it was. *So where was Dad?*

"If you've done something to him ..." she said to the house.

She heard laughter. *Was it in her head? Was it in the house? Maybe they were now the same thing?*

"I haven't done anything to him," the voice told her. "He's going to do something to you."

"He wouldn't. He's my father," Debbie screamed. "My dad!"

"Not any more," the voice said. "He belongs to me now."

"No, you're wrong. You killed Jane, didn't you? You took her body and threw her in the lake. You liked killing her, didn't you?"

Then Debbie knew where the walking stick was.

"You used it to break the ice, didn't you? So you could put Jane's body in the water."

There was more laughter. Sexton was enjoying this.

"What did you do? Did you weight her down with stones so she'd sink and they wouldn't find her?"

More evil, mocking laughter.

"So you came back for more. Even from the mental hospital, even from your grave. You kept coming back."

There was no voice now. There was no laughter.

Debbie searched the house. Her father wasn't there. Nor was the walking stick. Her skin was covered in gooseflesh. But she had to have one more look for him.

****

Debbie was in the attic where Dad had made tea when she felt the cold again. She saw the windowpane frost over. In the frosted glass something was forming. Eyes, a nose, a face framed by hair and a bonnet.

"Jane?" said Debbie.

Then the face was screaming. It was an awful, silent scream.

The glass cleared, the face faded and a moment later she saw through the window the reason for the scream. Dad was coming through the woods. In his right hand he was holding the walking stick. Jane had been warning her. As Dad moved through the woods the weather changed. A storm broke over the house. Thunder rolled through the sky and rain came down, heavy columns like iron. As Dad came closer Debbie saw his eyes. Cold, piggy eyes.

"Jane," he shouted hoarsely through the rain. "Where are you, girl?"

Debbie turned from the window but he had seen her. She ran to bolt the front door.

"Jane!" he shouted.

She fled through the hallway. As she reached the bottom of the stairs Dad kicked in the front door.

"Think you can lock me out of my own house, do you?"

She ran to the back door. She grabbed the handle. For the second time that day the cold burned into her hand. The house wouldn't let her out. In that moment she saw him.

"There you are, Jane."

"Dad, don't listen to him. I'm not Jane. I'm Debbie."

"Come here, Jane," he said.

"Dad, you've got to shut Sexton out."

"Jane, I order you to come with me."

She hesitated. Then he showed his rage. He smashed the silver tip of the walking stick down on the floor.

"Jane!"

Debbie started to run. She raced upstairs. She ran along the landing trying all the doors. Each of the handles was the same. They were all so cold they burned her skin. But one door was open. The door of the room with the mirror.

She saw Dad coming down the landing. There was only one way to go. She backed inside. "Please Dad, don't!" Debbie begged.

Dad walked in and closed the door behind him.

Chapter 12
Jane

Debbie saw Dad and herself in the mirror. But she was wearing a black dress, white apron and white bonnet. She was Jane. And Dad was standing facing her, wearing a tweed suit and holding a silver-tipped walking stick. He was James Sexton.

"Now for that lesson, Jane."

One last time Debbie pleaded with him.

"Dad, I'm not Jane and you're not James Sexton. He's evil. You must fight him."

But the look in his eyes told her he could not fight. He raised the walking stick. He was about to strike.

Debbie was beyond begging. She threw up her hands, closed her eyes and waited for the blow. But it didn't come. Debbie opened her eyes. She could still see herself and Dad in the mirror, but there was someone else.

It was the real Jane. It wasn't Jane in her maid's uniform. It was the Jane of the Mere. She was grey and lifeless, almost entirely covered with pondweed. But she was there, blocking Dad's way. Seventy years after dying at Sexton's hands, Jane was fighting back.

"Dad!" shouted Debbie.

The walking stick came down. But it didn't swing at her head. Jane had entered

Dad's mind and shut out Sexton. The stick smashed into the mirror. Debbie turned away to avoid the flying glass.

When she turned back Dad was staring at her, white-faced. "How did I get here?" he asked.

"Don't worry about that," said Debbie. "Are you all right?"

"I'm fine. But why am I all wet?"

"I'll tell you later."

"And why's the mirror smashed?"

Debbie smiled. "I'll tell you that later too. Let's go home. I'll tell you there."

As they walked from the room she noticed that it wasn't just the mirror which was smashed. The walking stick lay broken on the floor. Its power had gone. It was true of the whole house. Sexton had finally left it.

"I feel warm again," said Debbie.

The house wasn't a monster any more, it was just bricks and mortar. Dad opened the car door. He still looked confused. Just before she got in beside him, Debbie looked back at the house. There were no eyes staring down from the windows.

****

The next day Debbie and her dad were standing by the side of the Mere.

"I don't know how you can look at me just as if nothing had happened. I nearly killed you," said Dad.

"Dad, it wasn't you. It was Sexton."

"And he's gone?"

Debbie nodded. "Yes, he's gone forever. He won't hurt anybody ever again. You can do up the Grange for the lady from London and we can keep our house."

Dad stared out across the water. "Where did you see Jane?"

"Over there, by that crumbling wooden landing-stage."

"I wish there was some way to thank her," said Dad.

"We've already thanked her," said Debbie. "They've both been here all these years. She had to watch while he played his evil games with the others. But when we got rid of Sexton, we ended her nightmare."

"She saved us."

"Yes," said Debbie. "We wouldn't be here without her."

Without another word Debbie laid a wreath of red roses on the surface of the Mere. Together, she and her father watched it slowly drift away.

Barrington Stoke would like to thank all its readers for commenting on the manuscript before publication and in particular:

Donna Marie Ball	Becky Keogh
Chris Bangs	Marc McNaughton
Heather Boyd	Chantelle Millward
Catriona Campbell	Amanda Minns
Darren Campbell	Lewis Mitchell
Kevin Corcoran	Anas Mohyuddin
Kenneth Darby	Martin Payne
Matthew Dolan	Samantha Priest
Kathryn Edwards	Hilary Riches
Arron Ellis	Kieran Roze
Greg Flucker	Lynsey Smith
Melissa Geddes	Serena Steele
Andrew Gosling	Robert Steeples
Kevin Hart	Wendy Taylor
Richard Hinton	Hayley Upton
Jemma Jenkins	Thomas Walker
Anthony Kent	Paulette Worsey

Become a Consultant!

Would you like to give us feedback on our titles before they are published? Contact us at the e-mail address below – we'd love to hear from you!

E-mail: info@barringtonstoke.co.uk
Website: www.barringtonstoke.co.uk

More Teen Titles!

Barrington Stoke, 10 Belford Terrace, Edinburgh EH4 3DQ
Tel: 0131 315 4933 Fax: 0131 315 4934
E-mail: info@barringtonstoke.co.uk
Website: www.barringtonstoke.co.uk